I'm Game!

by Nancy Krulik • illustrated by John & Wendy

Grosset & Dunlap

For Mandy and Ian—NK
For Andrea, the Queen of
the Roller Derby—J&W

GROSSET & DUNLAP
Published by the Penguin Group
Penguin Group (USA) Inc., 375 Hudson Street,
New York, New York 10014, U.S.A.
Penguin Group (Canada), 90 Eglinton Avenue East, Suite 700,
Toronto, Ontario, Canada M4P 2Y3
(a division of Pearson Penguin Canada Inc.)
Penguin Books Ltd, 80 Strand, London WC2R 0RL, England
Penguin Ireland, 25 St Stephen's Green, Dublin 2, Ireland
(a division of Penguin Books Ltd)
Penguin Group (Australia), 250 Camberwell Road,
Camberwell, Victoria 3124, Australia
(a division of Pearson Australia Group Pty Ltd)
Penguin Books India Pvt Ltd, 11 Community Centre,
Panchsheel Park, New Delhi - 110 017, India
Penguin Group (NZ), Cnr Airborne and Rosedale Roads,
Albany, Auckland 1310, New Zealand
(a division of Pearson New Zealand Ltd)
Penguin Books (South Africa) (Pty) Ltd, 24 Sturdee Avenue,
Rosebank, Johannesburg 2196, South Africa

Penguin Books Ltd, Registered Offices:
80 Strand, London WC2R 0RL, England

Library of Congress Control Number: 2005037078

ISBN 0-448-44133-0 10 9 8 7 6 5 4 3 2 1

Chapter 1

"Hurry up, Daddy, it's starting!" Katie Carew shouted. She turned on the television set in the living room just as the familiar theme music began to play.

"Welcome to *Tick, Tock, Clock*, the game show that pits speed against smarts!" the show's star, Bob Ritchey, said.

"Did I miss anything?" Mr. Carew asked as he leaped onto the couch beside Katie.

"Just the song," Katie assured him. She knew her dad hated missing even a minute of his favorite TV game show.

Katie liked *Tick, Tock, Clock* a lot, too. The questions they asked were usually too hard for her, but she liked watching what happened when the contestants answered incorrectly. They had to do all kinds of weird things in order to stay in the game, like fill a bucket with milk—using only their cupped hands to carry the milk across the stage.

Or search around with their mouths in a big bowl of goo to find a jellybean.

Or catch water balloons on a spoon while they rode on a unicycle.

Or slither through a maze on their bellies like a snake.

The hardest part was that the contestants had to finish their stunt before the Tick Tock Clock buzzed. If they didn't, they were out of the game.

"Name the capital of New York State," Bob Ritchey asked the contestants.

"Albany," Katie's father replied right away. He smiled confidently. "That was an easy one."

Katie smiled proudly at her dad. "You'd win if you were on the show," she said.

Mr. Carew grinned. "Probably. When it comes to answering questions, I'm the champ."

"Here at home you are," Katie's mom teased as she sat down on the couch. "But I'll bet it's not that easy when you're playing against two other people and you have those TV cameras staring at you."

Mr. Carew shrugged and listened to Bob Ritchey's next question.

"Whose picture is on the one hundred dollar bill?" Bob asked the contestants.

"Benjamin Franklin," Katie's father shouted out.

The contestant on TV said, "President Kennedy."

"Sorry, that's incorrect," Bob Ritchey told the woman on TV. "The correct answer is Benjamin Franklin."

Mr. Carew nodded. "Told ya," he said.

Katie and her parents watched as the contestant spun a big wheel. There were six pictures on the wheel: a snake, a bowl of

green goo, a chicken, a unicycle, and a cow with a milk pail.

"I wonder what stunt she'll get," Katie said.

The wheel went round and round and finally stopped on the picture of a chicken.

Bob Ritchey grinned. "You know what that means," he said to the audience as he handed the woman a pair of roller skates, a raincoat, and a rain hat. The rain hat had a glass bowl attached to it.

Katie giggled as the woman put on the hat. "Boy, she looks funny."

Bob Ritchey pointed up. There were three large cardboard chickens swaying overhead from the ceiling.

"Those are the *Tick, Tock, Clock* chickens," Bob explained to the woman. "As soon as I say 'go,' they will start laying eggs. You have one minute to skate around and catch five eggs in the bowl on the top of your head." He paused and smiled at the camera. "On your mark. Get set. Go!"

Suddenly an egg fell from one chicken and then another. It was hard to tell which chicken would lay the next egg. The woman started skating, trying to catch them in her hat.

She wasn't very good at it. She kept missing. Raw eggs splattered on the floor. Egg slime sloshed all over her.

"No wonder they gave her a raincoat," Mrs. Carew noted.

"This is a really hard stunt," Mr. Carew said.

Katie turned and smiled at her dad. "It would be so great if you could be on the show. I'm sure you would win lots of prizes."

"I know," Mr. Carew replied sadly. "But *Tick, Tock, Clock* is filmed in Hollywood. There's no way I can ever be on it."

Katie frowned. That just didn't seem fair.

Chapter 2

"Woohoo!" Mr. Carew shouted the next morning. He was reading the newspaper at the breakfast table. "I don't believe it."

"What?" Katie and her mom asked him at the same time.

"*Tick, Tock, Clock,*" Mr. Carew replied. "The show is going on a tour. They will be filming in different cities all over the country. And on Friday they're going to be here!"

"In Cherrydale?" Katie's mother exclaimed. "*This* Friday?"

"Daddy, you have to get on the show!" Katie cried out.

"This article gives a phone number you can

call to try out," Mr. Carew told her.

"How can you try out over the telephone?" Katie asked her dad.

"It says here that there will be four questions you have to answer," Mr. Carew read. "If you answer four correctly, then you may be picked to be on *Tick, Tock, Clock.*"

"Call right away!" Katie shouted. "I'll bet half of the people in Cherrydale are calling that phone number right now."

Mr. Carew leaped up and ran to the phone.

"Katie, please go get your backpack," Mrs. Carew said. "I'll drive you to school on my way to work."

"But I want to see if Daddy can answer those four questions," Katie pleaded.

"Sorry," her mom said. "We've got to get going or I'll be late."

Katie frowned, but she hurried upstairs. Her chocolate and white cocker spaniel, Pepper, nipped at her heels as she ran.

"Wouldn't it be so exciting if Daddy got to

be on TV?" Katie asked Pepper as she slipped her math worksheet into her homework folder.

Pepper smiled and wagged his tail excitedly. Katie grinned. Sometimes she was sure that her dog understood everything she said.

"See you later," Katie told Pepper. Then she raced back to the kitchen. "Mom, I'm ready," she said.

Her mother was standing at the kitchen door. "Shhh . . ." she whispered. Mrs. Carew pointed to the phone. "Daddy's answering those questions for the test."

Katie could hardly believe it!

"Madagascar," Katie's father said into the phone.

Katie crossed her fingers and her toes. She hoped it was the right answer.

"Yes!" Mr. Carew shouted suddenly.

Katie grinned.

"That's the third one he got right," Mrs. Carew whispered to Katie. "One more to go!"

Katie's heart beat hard as her father listened to the last question. "How do cows sleep?" he repeated. "Hmm . . . standing up?"

Katie bit her lip nervously.

Was that the right answer?

Suddenly, a huge smile spread across Katie's father's face. "Wow!" he shouted excitedly. "That's great. Okay. Friday evening at six thirty. I'll be there."

After he hung up the phone, Katie's dad hugged her mom. "I don't believe it. I made it!" he shouted. "This is incredible. I'm going to be on *Tick, Tock, Clock*!"

"I guess wishes do come true," Mrs. Carew said with a smile.

Katie gulped. Her mother was right. Wishes did come true. Unfortunately, it wasn't always so great when they did.

Chapter 3

Katie knew all about wishes—especially the kind that came true. One of *her* wishes had come true—and it kept on coming true over and over again.

It had all started one horrible day back in third grade. Katie had lost the ball game for her team. Then she'd splashed mud all over her favorite jeans. But the worst part of the day came when Katie let out a loud burp—right in front of the whole class. It had been so embarrassing!

That night, Katie made a wish that she could be anyone but herself. There must have been a shooting star overhead when she made the wish, because the very next day the magic wind came.

The magic wind was a really powerful tornado that blew only around Katie. It was so strong, it could blow her right out of her body . . . *and into someone else's*!

The first time the magic wind blew, it turned Katie into Speedy, the hamster in her third-grade classroom. Katie spent the whole morning running round and round on a hamster wheel and chewing on Speedy's wooden chew sticks. They didn't taste very good at all.

The magic wind had come back many times after that. Each time it turned her into somebody new—her best friends, Jeremy and Suzanne, her third-grade teacher, Mrs. Derkman, and even Pepper. That had been *really* weird—Katie had to go to the bathroom by lifting her leg up on a fire hydrant.

The switcheroo never lasted very long. It went as suddenly as it came, which was a good thing. Because every time Katie turned into somebody else, that person seemed to land in big trouble!

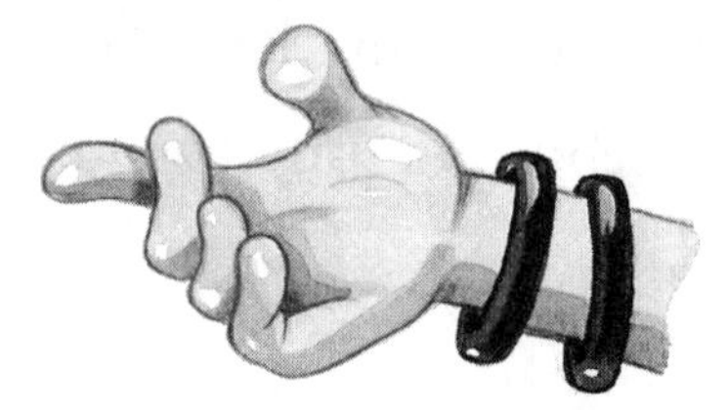

Chapter 4

Katie couldn't wait to tell her friends all about her dad being on TV. But when she got to the school playground, everyone was clustered around George.

"George, those are so cool," she heard Mandy Banks say. "Where did you get them?"

Katie walked over to where a group of fourth-graders were standing. Everyone was staring at something, but Katie couldn't get close enough to see what it was.

"What's so cool?" she asked her best friend Suzanne Lock.

Suzanne sighed. "George got some rubber bracelets. Everyone's going nuts over them. I don't know why."

Katie shrugged. Suzanne was never excited about anything that made someone else the center of attention.

"*You* look happy," Suzanne said, noticing the big smile on Katie's face.

"The greatest thing happened!" Katie told her. "My dad's going to be on *Tick, Tock, Clock*! He found out this morning."

"No way!" Suzanne exclaimed.

"Really," Katie assured her. "They're going to be filming in Cherrydale and my dad is going to be one of the contestants."

"Wow! Your dad's going to be on TV!" Suzanne shouted, loud enough for the other kids to hear.

Suddenly, the fourth-graders turned away from George. They all looked at Suzanne and Katie.

Katie was impressed. Suzanne really was something.

"What show is your dad going to be on,

Katie?" Jeremy Fox asked.

"*Tick, Tock, Clock,*" Suzanne answered before Katie could say anything. "He just found out this morning. And *I* was the first person Katie told."

Katie sighed. Suzanne was obviously trying to make Jeremy think that Katie liked her better. And that wasn't true.

"Where did you get those?" Katie asked George.

"At the skateboard park," George replied. "But you can also buy them at Hot Stuff in the mall."

Katie knew the store. If there was anything new and cool to buy, Hot Stuff had it!

"Maybe your dad should wear one for luck when he's on *Tick, Tock, Clock,*" George suggested to Katie.

"Oh please, George," Suzanne said, rolling her eyes. "Why would Katie's father want to wear a stupid piece of rubber on his wrist?"

"*I* think they're cool," Kevin said. "I want

to get some."

"Me too," Emma Weber said.

Suzanne scowled and walked away.

Katie felt kind of bad for her friend. Usually it was Suzanne who set trends at Cherrydale Elementary School. She wasn't happy that everyone wanted to get bracelets like George's.

Chapter 5

"Hey there, Katie!" Mr. Carew greeted his daughter as he walked into the back office of the Book Nook bookstore late that afternoon.

Katie's mom was the manager of the Book Nook. Katie often came to the mall after school to do her homework in the back office while her mom worked.

"Daddy, what are you doing here?" Katie asked as she looked up from her math sheet.

"I left work early. I want to do a little research," he explained.

Katie knew what research was. She did research projects in school. You had to look up all kinds of facts and then write a paper about them.

"Are you writing a report?" Katie asked her father.

Mr. Carew shook his head. "Actually, I wanted to buy a book of facts so I can study for the show."

"What kind of facts?" Katie asked him.

"All kinds. Facts about places, people, sports, science, medicine, history, and all the other things they ask questions about on *Tick, Tock, Clock*."

Just then Katie's mother entered the office. She was holding a thick book.

"Here you go, honey," Mrs. Carew told her husband. "This is the best trivia book we have."

"What's trivia?" Katie asked.

"Interesting facts that most people don't know," her mom explained. She opened the book and read a fact. "Did you know

that sneezes travel out of your mouth at about one hundred miles per hour?"

Katie made a face. "That's gross," she said.

"But it's a fact," her mom replied. "And this book is full of them!"

"Soon my mind will be full of them, too!" Katie's dad added with a grin as he took the book from his wife.

X X X

A little while later when Katie and her father went to Louie's Pizza Parlor, they found Suzanne sitting at a table. Suzanne was concentrating on something she was holding in her hands. She didn't even notice Katie and her dad.

"Hello, Suzanne," Katie said, waving a hand in front of her friend's face.

"Oh, hi, Katie. Hi, Mr. Carew," Suzanne replied, looking up. "Sorry. I was making something."

"What?" Katie asked her.

Suzanne held up a black rubber bracelet.

It was just like George's, except it had a thin strip of pink ribbon twisted around it. Now the bracelet had pink and black stripes, like some sort of funky candy cane.

"That's so pretty," Katie told her.

"I've already made seven of them," Suzanne replied. "That's two more bracelets than George has."

Katie sighed. Suzanne always had to be better than everyone else.

"This one is for you," Suzanne said, handing Katie the finished bracelet. "Because you're my best friend."

"Wow! Thanks," Katie said sincerely as she slipped it on her wrist.

Just then, Louie walked over to the table. "Hi, everyone. What'll it be?"

"Do you have the broccoli and mushroom pizza today?" Katie asked hopefully. "I want my dad to try it."

"I've got one coming out of the oven in a minute," Louie assured her.

"Guess what? My dad is going to be on *Tick, Tock, Clock*!" Katie said proudly. Then using her new vocabulary word, she added, "He just bought a trivia book to help him."

Mr. Carew leaned back in his chair. "I don't really *need* the book," he told Louie. "I'm already a whiz at the kinds of questions they ask on the show."

"I love *Tick, Tock, Clock*," Louie told Katie's dad. "Do you think you'll wind up with green goo all over you?"

"Oh, I doubt that will happen," Katie's dad replied. "I'm going to just zip through the questions. I've got tons of information floating around in my head. Go ahead, ask me anything."

"Okay," Louie said. "How about . . . What was the name of the first pizza parlor in North America?"

"Lombardi's," Mr. Carew answered. "In New York City. It opened in 1905."

"Wow, you *are* good!" Louie exclaimed.

"I told you," Mr. Carew agreed. "I'm going to win. I can feel it."

Chapter 6

When Katie arrived at school on Wednesday morning, it looked as though the entire fourth grade were being attacked by skinny black snakes. Everyone was wearing black rubber bracelets.

Jeremy was wearing nine of them. So were George and Kevin.

Kadeem was wearing eight bracelets, just like Mandy and Becky.

Suzanne's striped ones really stood out, though.

"Wow, your bracelets are cool," Jessica Haynes told Suzanne. "How many do you have?"

Suzanne frowned. "Six," she said slowly. Then her face brightened suddenly. "But mine are extra-special. I made them myself. Katie has one, too. I made it for her."

Katie held up her wrist. Once again, Suzanne had them all beat. And once again she was bragging about it.

X X X

Suzanne wasn't the only one bragging these days.

That evening, Katie and her dad sat outside on the front porch. Katie had the trivia book on her lap.

"What is the national bird of the United States?" she asked her father.

"That's easy! The bald eagle," Mr. Carew replied. "Although some people once wanted our national bird to be a turkey!"

Katie giggled. That was a funny thought.

"But I'm no turkey," her dad said. "I'm a trivia *genius*."

Katie frowned slightly. She didn't like when

anyone bragged—not even her dad.

"Hey there," Katie's next-door neighbors, Mr. and Mrs. Derkman, greeted them.

Katie sat up tall as the Derkmans walked across the lawn toward her house. When Mrs. Derkman had been Katie's third-grade teacher, she'd always told the kids to sit up straight. Mrs. Derkman wasn't Katie's teacher anymore. But Katie still sat up straight when she saw her.

"So, are you getting ready for the big show on Friday?" Mr. Derkman asked Katie's dad.

"I'm testing him," Katie said proudly. "He's doing great!"

"I'm a cinch to win," Mr. Carew boasted. "Haven't missed one yet."

"Are you going to practice the stunts?" Mrs. Derkman asked.

"Nah. That won't be necessary," Katie's dad assured her.

Katie hoped her dad was right. He didn't even know *how* to roller-skate, never mind ride a unicycle.

"Try me," her father said.

Mrs. Derkman thought for a moment. "Here's one I learned when we took a trip to Australia," she said. "What is the largest species of kangaroo?"

"The red kangaroo," Mr. Carew said confidently.

Mrs. Derkman looked impressed. "Correct," she said.

“I’ve got one,” Mr. Derkman said. “Who do mosquitoes bite more—kids or adults?”

Katie thought she knew the answer to that one. After all, she got bitten by mosquitoes all the time.

“Adults,” her dad answered.

“Right,” Mr. Derkman told him.

Katie would have been wrong. But her dad wasn’t. He’d done it again!

“I’m telling you, I can’t lose,” Mr. Carew boasted.

“Daddy!” Katie exclaimed, embarrassed.

“I hope you’re right,” Mr. Derkman told him. “The whole neighborhood will be cheering you on. Everyone’s going to be watching you on Friday night.”

“Doesn’t that make you nervous, Daddy?” she asked. “There are going to be millions of people all over the country listening to every-thing you say. Millions and millions of them. And they’re going to be looking right at you when you try to give an answer. I’d be a wreck if I had to do that."

"Um, no, I won't be . . . well . . ." Mr. Carew told her. "I mean . . . I hadn't really thought about it that way before. I'll just focus on the questions."

Katie frowned. Suddenly her dad sounded kind of nervous.

"That's exactly right. Just keep studying," Mrs. Derkman assured Katie's dad. "Don't worry about anything else. You know this stuff."

Katie smiled at Mrs. Derkman. When she wasn't being a very strict third-grade teacher, she could be kind of nice.

Mr. Carew nodded. But he didn't seem nearly as excited as before. He was obviously thinking about how many people would be watching him. Katie never should have brought it up. She felt awful. She had to do something to make sure her father could get his confidence back.

But what?

Chapter 7

Katie's dad spent the whole night walking around the house memorizing facts. He was starting to make Katie and her mom a little crazy.

When Katie woke up in the morning and went downstairs for breakfast, she found her dad sitting at the kitchen table with his trivia book and a giant mug of coffee. His eyes were all red, and he hadn't shaven yet.

"Hawaii is made up of twenty islands," he mumbled. "Ancient Egyptians slept on pillows made of stone. China has the most people in the world."

He sounded like a zombie.

Things were pretty crazy at school, too. Everyone was arguing about whose rubber bracelets were the best. The boys all had plain black ones. The girls were all copying Suzanne and wearing black bracelets with colored ribbons wrapped around them.

Suzanne had created a rainbow on her arms. Bracelets with red, orange, yellow, green, blue, and violet ribbons ran up and down both of her arms.

Katie was still wearing the one bracelet Suzanne had made for her. She had been so busy helping her father study for *Tick, Tock, Clock* she hadn't had time to buy any more.

"I think it's a lucky bracelet for me," Katie told Suzanne that afternoon as the girls stood together in the cafeteria lunch line. "I got a 98 on my math quiz today. And yesterday, when I was practicing on my clarinet, I played *Yankee Doodle* all the way through without hitting one wrong note."

Suzanne smiled. "Glad I could help."

"You must be having *lots* of good luck with all those bracelets you are wearing," Katie told her friend.

"Not exactly," Suzanne admitted. "It's been kind of the opposite, actually. The spelling worksheet I handed in this morning was a mess. Every time I started to write something down, the rubber part of the bracelets would tear the paper."

Katie nodded. Suzanne wasn't the only

one having problems with her bracelets. All morning long the little black bands of rubber had been causing trouble for people.

During math, Mr. Guthrie scolded Kadeem for playing with his bracelets instead of paying attention.

In physical education, George dropped the ball because having so many bracelets made it hard for him to move his wrist.

The worst was at lunch . . .

"Ouch!" Becky Stern shouted from the lunch line. She turned around and stared at a rubber bracelet on the floor and then at a group of boys behind her.

"Which one of you hit me with that bracelet?" she demanded.

"Not me," George assured her.

"It wasn't me," Kevin added.

"Me neither," Kadeem said.

"Well, it was one of you," Becky insisted. "And I'm going to get you back," she said. She took off one of her pink and black bracelets

and shot it at George.

George shot a bracelet back at Becky. She ducked. The bracelet hit Mandy in the arm instead.

"Ow!" Mandy shouted. Then she pulled a bracelet from her arm and shot it at George. It hit Kevin instead.

"Oh, you're gonna get it!" Kevin declared, pulling off a bracelet and shooting it in Mandy's direction.

Instead of hitting Mandy, he got Miriam Chan in the back of the head. She dropped her tray in surprise.

"Oh no!" Miriam cried out as pasta, tomato sauce, and orange juice splashed all over the floor.

"What is going on here?" Mr. Kane, the principal, demanded, running over to the lunch line.

Mr. Kane didn't see the pool of slippery tomato sauce. *Whoosh!* He flew up in the air and then landed on the floor with a thud.

"That's it!" Mr. Kane shouted. He pulled himself up and wiped tomato sauce and pudding from the seat of his pants. "From now on, there will be no rubber bracelets worn in school!"

Suzanne frowned. "I worked so hard making all of these," she whispered to Katie. "What am I supposed to do with them now?"

Katie shook her head. She had no idea.

But Katie knew exactly what to do with hers. She was sure *her* bracelet was a lucky one! She would do what George had suggested to her earlier in the week. She would give her bracelet to her father. He could wear it for luck when he was on TV.

A good luck charm would guarantee that her dad would do well on the show. Now he would have no reason to be nervous at all!

Chapter 8

"The Tick Tock Clock looks so much bigger on TV," Katie said as she settled into a seat in the TV studio on Friday night.

"I guess it's just the camera angles that make everything look big on TV," Katie's mom replied.

Katie looked around. There sure were a lot of cameras. They were placed all around the stage. Katie hoped they didn't block her view of her dad.

Katie was too excited to sit still. She turned around and waved to Mr. and Mrs. Fox. They had gotten tickets to the show and were there to cheer Katie's dad on.

"Why did Daddy have to go backstage already?" Katie asked her mom. "The show doesn't start for a while."

"They had to put a microphone on him, and do his hair and makeup," her mom explained.

"Do you think they'll make Daddy wear lipstick?" Katie asked her mother.

Mrs. Carew smiled. "Imagine him with bright red lips," she joked.

"Now *that* would be funny," Katie said with a giggle.

It was getting kind of noisy in the studio now. The seats in the audience were filling up. The show was completely sold out. Katie wasn't surprised. It wasn't every day that a big show like *Tick, Tock, Clock* came to Cherrydale!

The people without tickets would also be watching. Louie had set up a TV right in the middle of his restaurant.

Cinnamon, the woman who owned the

candy store in the Cherrydale Mall, had a TV, too—and she was giving out candy watches to anyone who came by to watch *Tick, Tock, Clock* with her.

Mr. and Mrs. Derkman had promised not to miss the show. They were going to watch it with Mr. Brigandi, another of Katie's neighbors.

Katie's friends had all promised to get their homework done really early so they could be allowed to watch TV.

Katie was very proud. She couldn't wait for everyone to see how smart her dad was.

But the waiting was getting harder and harder. Katie looked at the Tick Tock Clock. Only five minutes to go.

"I wish the show would start already," Katie told her mother.

"I know," Mrs. Carew agreed. "I'm getting so jittery just sitting here. I hope your father is trying to stay calm. Last night he was so nervous he was shouting out facts in his sleep."

Katie frowned. Her dad had been a bundle of nerves ever since Katie had reminded him about how many people would be watching him on TV.

"Cross your fingers, honey, to give Daddy good luck," Mrs. Carew said.

Good luck.

Oh, no! She'd forgotten to give her father his good luck charm. She couldn't let him go onstage without that! Quickly she leaped up from her seat.

"Katie, where are you going?" Mrs. Carew asked her.

"I have to give something to Daddy!" Katie replied as she ran toward the backstage area.

"You can't go back there!" Mrs. Carew shouted after her.

But Katie didn't listen. She had to reach her daddy in time!

Chapter 9

The people backstage were all very busy. They were talking to each other through their headsets as they ran around checking on wires and lights and things. They were all too focused on their work to even notice the redheaded fourth-grade girl who had slipped backstage.

Katie was glad of that. She didn't want to get sent back to her seat. Katie just had to find her father!

"Two minutes till showtime," she heard one of the women say into her headset. "Let's get the three contestants onstage."

Oh, no! Katie didn't see her father anywhere. In fact, she didn't see *anyone* who looked like a contestant. The only people around were the folks with the headsets and clipboards.

Quickly Katie hurried down an empty hallway lined with doors. "Daddy!" she called out, knocking on the first door. "Are you in there?"

Katie waited for a reply. There was no answer.

"Daddy, it's me, Katie," she said, knocking on the second door.

Again, there was no answer.

"Sixty seconds till showtime," she heard the woman shout.

As Katie looked around frantically, she felt a cool breeze blowing on the back of her neck. She pulled her blazer around her tightly.

But that didn't make her any warmer. A wool blazer was no match for this wind. *This* was the magic wind.

Uh-oh!

Within seconds, the magic wind began to

blow harder and harder. It circled around Katie like a tornado.

"Oh, no! Not now, please!" Katie cried out as the magic wind blew wildly around her.

Katie wanted to cry. She didn't want to switcheroo—especially not now. Not when her daddy was about to be on TV!

And then, suddenly, it stopped. Just like that. The magic wind was gone.

And so was Katie. She'd been turned into someone else . . . switcheroo!

The question was, *who*?

Chapter 10

Slowly, Katie opened her eyes. She looked down at her shoes. Her red shoes were gone. Brown loafers were on her feet now.

She wasn't wearing her black and white skirt and blazer, either. Instead she had on a pair of light brown slacks and a pale blue shirt.

Katie knew that shirt well. She'd helped pick it out . . . *for her father*!

Katie gulped nervously. She looked around. She was behind a wooden stand. There was a blue buzzer on the stand by her right hand.

There was a woman standing on one side

of her and a man on the other. They were both behind wooden stands, too.

"Uh-oh," Katie murmured.

"Thanks, Mr. Carew," one of the women with a headset replied. "Your microphone is working perfectly."

Mr. Carew! Yikes! Katie had turned into her father—right before he was supposed to go on TV!

"Thirty seconds until showtime!" the woman with the headset shouted.

This was *so* not good!

Just then Bob Ritchey walked onto the set. He turned to one of his assistants. "Is my hair on straight?" he asked her.

"Move it a little to the left, Bob," she told him.

Bob Ritchey shifted his toupee slightly.

Katie couldn't believe it. "You wear a wig?" she exclaimed. Then she blushed.

But Bob Ritchey didn't mind. "Sure do," he said. "And I always have to fix it before the show goes on the air." He looked at Katie's head. "You might want to try one yourself, Dave," he said, calling Katie by her father's name. "Your hair is getting a little thin on top there!"

Everyone in the audience laughed. All except Katie's mother, that is. She was glancing around nervously. Katie knew she was looking for her. But there was nothing Katie could do. She was stuck here.

Just then red lights appeared on all of the cameras. That meant the show was starting. Music began to play, and Bob Ritchey moved to the front of the stage.

"Welcome to *Tick, Tock, Clock*, the game show that pits speed against smarts!" he said.

The audience clapped.

"Tonight we're coming to you from the town of Cherrydale!" Bob Ritchey continued with a big smile.

Suddenly everyone in the audience began cheering wildly.

"Woohoo!"

"Oh yeah!"

"Cherrydale rocks!"

"Wow! What a great group you are," Bob Ritchey told the audience. Then he turned to the three contestants. "Are you all ready to play?"

Katie gulped. She was definitely not ready to play. Not at all. It was her father who knew all those trivia facts. Those were things grown-ups knew. But Katie wasn't a grown-up. She was just a nine-year-old girl.

A nine-year-old girl who was about to make a fool of herself on national TV!

Chapter 11

"Okay, let's meet our three contestants," Bob Ritchey continued. He walked over to the woman on Katie's left. "Tell us a little bit about yourself and your family," he said.

"My name is Elaine Blackwell," the woman answered. "I'm single. I'm a doctor at Cherrydale Hospital, and in my spare time I like to skydive."

"Wow, you must be very brave," Bob Ritchey said, sounding very impressed.

"Nothing scares me," Elaine assured him.

"Not even the Tick Tock Clock?" Bob asked her.

Elaine shook her head confidently.

Bob walked over and stood in front of Katie. "Dave Carew," he said. "Tell us about yourself."

Katie took a deep breath. "Well, um, I live in Cherrydale with my mom . . ." Katie gulped. She was supposed to be her dad! "I mean with my *wife*, Wendy, and my daughter, Katie."

"And where do you work?" Bob Ritchey asked her.

"In an office," Katie told him.

"What kind of office?" Bob Ritchey wondered.

"I'm not sure," Katie replied nervously. She could feel her cheeks getting red.

"You're not sure what you do for a living?" Bob Ritchey asked, surprised.

The audience began to laugh. Katie blushed harder.

"Um. I think I do something with computers," Katie told him.

Bob Ritchey looked at her strangely. The audience's laughter grew louder. Katie's mother looked puzzled.

Katie was so embarrassed, she didn't hear anything the third and final contestant, Arthur Somebody, said about himself. She was too busy thinking about how silly she'd just made herself look.

Or her *dad* look, actually. And that was worse!

"Okay, contestants, you know the rules," Bob Ritchey said. "When you know the answer, hit the button. But be sure you really know it; otherwise, things can get really messy!" Bob Ritchey pointed to the stunt wheel. The audience laughed. They knew what that meant.

"Okay, here's your first question," Bob said. "Which is heavier, milk or cream?"

Hmm . . . Katie thought. Cream felt heavier than milk when you drank it. She reached for the buzzer.

Suddenly, she noticed a camera with a red light. It was pointed right on her.

Katie was on TV!

All she could do was stare at that red light.

She was frozen.

Beep. Elaine pressed her buzzer. "Milk," she shouted.

"You're right!" Bob Ritchey cheered. "Next question. How many points are there on the Statue of Liberty's crown?"

Katie knew that one! She'd read it in her dad's book. She reached for her buzzer and . . .

Beep. Elaine hit her buzzer first.

"Seven, Bob," she said.

"Right again, Elaine," Bob Ritchey replied. "Let's see if you can make it three for three. Where is the red light on a traffic light located—on the top or on the bottom?"

Beep. This time it was Arthur who pushed his buzzer first.

"The bottom," Arthur said confidently.

Bob Ritchey sighed heavily. "I'm sorry. That's wrong," he said. "A red light is always located on top." He smiled at the audience.

"But you still have a chance to stay in the game. All you have to do is . . ."

"Beat the Tick Tock Clock!" the audience shouted out in one voice.

"We'll find out what your challenge is as soon as we come back from this commercial break," Bob Ritchey told Arthur.

At that moment, the red light turned off. Katie breathed a sigh of relief.

Well, at least I didn't answer anything wrong, she thought to herself.

Of course, she hadn't answered anything *right,* either.

Chapter 12

The wheel stopped on the picture of the snake when Arthur spun it. That meant Arthur had to wiggle his way through a slimy, greasy maze on his belly. He put on a yellow slicker that made him look like a banana.

The Tick Tock Clock started to count down.

"Come on, Arthur, slide!" Bob Ritchey shouted excitedly. "You can do it!"

Arthur was sliding all over the place on his belly. "Whoa!" he shouted as he tried to push himself uphill on the part of the maze that was like a slide. "Whoa!"

"Only five more seconds!" Bob Ritchey warned.

"Whoops!" Arthur exclaimed as he slid backward.

"Five . . . four . . . three . . . two . . . one!" the audience shouted.

The buzzer sounded.

"I'm sorry, Arthur," Bob Ritchey said. "But the Tick Tock Clock has spoken. I'm afraid you're out of the game."

Arthur struggled to stand up and shake Bob's hand. "Whoa!" he shouted again as he slipped and landed back on his belly again.

Bob Ritchey laughed and walked back over to where Katie and Elaine were standing.

"Okay, we're down to you two," he said. "Here's your next question: What bird moves the fastest?"

Before Katie could even think, she heard Elaine's buzzer ring.

"The ostrich, Bob," Elaine said proudly.

"You're right," Bob Ritchey cheered. He turned to Katie. "Come on, Dave. You have a lot of catching up to do."

Katie frowned. He wasn't kidding. Couldn't she get at least one question right? Her dad was looking like a fool in front of everybody.

"What does Popeye eat to get strong?" Bob Ritchey asked.

Katie smiled. She knew that one. Instantly she slammed her hand down on the buzzer. *Beep.*

Suddenly, all the cameras turned in Katie's direction. The red lights were all focused on her. She stared at them and smiled. Her lips felt glued together.

"Do you have an answer, Dave?" Bob Ritchey asked.

"Um . . . spaghetti!" Katie blurted out.

Immediately, the studio audience started laughing.

"Sorry, that's wrong," Bob Ritchey told Katie. "The correct answer is spinach! Popeye eats spinach to get strong."

Katie bit her lip. She couldn't believe it. She had given the wrong answer to the world's easiest question! Even Suzanne's baby sister would have known that one! Katie wanted to crawl offstage.

"But don't worry, Dave," Bob Ritchey continued. "You can still stay in the game. As long as you can beat the . . ."

"Tick Tock Clock," the audience chanted.

Then an alarm clock went off. "Oh, we're out of time." Bob Ritchey turned and smiled into the camera. "Dave's challenge will have to wait until Monday."

Chapter 13

"Okay, Bob, that's a wrap," one of the people with the headsets called out.

The stage lights turned off. Bob Ritchey headed backstage. Elaine looked at Katie and said, "Gee, I guess you were really nervous."

Katie couldn't even answer. It was like she was frozen in place.

As the audience began filing out of the studio, Katie watched her mother jump out of her seat and hurry backstage. Katie knew her mother was worried about her. After all, she'd disappeared half an hour ago.

But there was nothing Katie could do about that. She was stuck inside her father's body and she couldn't get out until the magic wind came back.

Katie raced off the stage in embarrassment and headed for a nearby bathroom. She stood there for a moment, alone by the sink, and stared into the mirror.

How could she have said "spaghetti"? Now people all over the country would think her dad wasn't very smart. She sure had made a mess of things this time.

Suddenly, Katie felt a cool breeze blowing on the back of her neck. She looked up to see if maybe she was standing beneath an air-conditioning vent.

But she wasn't. And there was no fan, either.

Which could mean only one thing!

The magic wind grew stronger now, spinning around and around, circling Katie like a wild tornado.

And then it stopped.

Just like that.

The magic wind was gone. Katie Carew was back . . .

But where was her dad? He was probably pretty upset right now. Katie raced out of the bathroom to look for him.

Mr. Carew was still standing on the stage. As Katie came near him, he blinked his eyes a few times and scratched his head.

"What are you doing here?" he asked her. Then he looked around at the empty stage. "Come to think of it, what am *I* doing here?"

"Don't you remember?" Katie asked him nervously.

"I remember someone putting makeup on me," Mr. Carew said. "And I sort of recall having a microphone attached to my shirt. But after that, it's all kind of fuzzy."

"You were playing the game," Katie told him.

"Oh," Mr. Carew replied. He frowned. "How'd I do?"

"Not too well," Katie admitted. "You have to do a stunt on Monday's show to stay in the game."

"Oh, no! That's it. I'm finished . . ." Mr.

Carew began. Then he stopped and looked at Katie curiously. "I seem to remember saying that Popeye ate spaghetti. Did I really do that?"

Katie nodded sadly.

"Why would I say that?" he wondered. "I know the answer's spinach."

"You were really nervous, Daddy," Katie told him. "Anybody would be. When those cameras swing around and the red lights stare at you, it's really scary!"

"You sound like you know exactly what it's like," Mr. Carew said.

Katie didn't answer him. What could she say?

"Katie! There you are!" Katie's mom exclaimed as she came running onto the stage. "Where did you disappear to?"

"I . . . um . . . I kind of got lost when I went backstage to find Daddy," she told her mom.

"Well, I'm just glad you're safe," her mother said, giving her a hug. Then she turned to

Katie's dad. "You'll do better on Monday, honey," she said.

"I don't know how that happened," Mr. Carew said, shaking his head.

"It's okay, Daddy. You're going to stay in the game," Katie assured him. "And you're going to come back and win!"

"How am I going to do that?" Mr. Carew asked her. "All the stunts look so hard."

Katie smiled brightly. She had just gotten one of her great ideas!

"Just leave everything to me," she assured him.

Chapter 14

"Okay, Mr. C., now lift your left leg up and put it in front of your right leg," George Brennan shouted as he watched Katie's dad try to roller-skate. "And don't forget to glide."

"I c-c-can't," Mr. Carew said nervously. Both his arms spun like pinwheels at his sides. "I'll fall."

"No, you won't," George assured him. "You just have to balance."

Mr. Carew slowly lifted his left leg off the ground. He moved it about two inches in front of his right leg and tried to glide. But then his skates seemed to keep on moving while the rest of him didn't.

Splat! He fell backward on his rear end.

"That's okay, Daddy," Katie assured him. "You'll get the hang of it."

"Sure you will," George agreed. But he didn't sound nearly as certain as Katie.

Neither did any of the other kids gathered at the playground on Saturday. Instead of their usual cooking club meeting, Katie, George, Jeremy, Kevin, Suzanne, and Becky were helping Mr. Carew practice for his next appearance on *Tick, Tock, Clock*.

The kids didn't know which of the six stunts the wheel would land on Monday night, so they were trying to get Mr. Carew ready for all of them. Right now, he was trying to do the *Tick, Tock, Clock* chicken stunt.

"Maybe he should try without skates first," Becky Stern called from a branch on a tree at the edge of the playground.

"That's an idea," Mr. Carew agreed. He began to open the laces on his skates.

"Okay." Katie turned to Suzanne. "Do you have the hat for Daddy?"

Suzanne nodded. "I used extra-strong glue to attach the bowl to this baseball cap," she told Katie proudly. "It won't ever come off."

Mr. Carew looked at the hat. "Oh, no.

That's my lucky baseball cap!" Katie's dad exclaimed.

Suzanne shrugged. "Sorry. It was the first one I saw in your front closet."

"It's all right," Katie assured her dad. "You'll be able to buy plenty of hats when you win."

"I guess," her dad replied as he placed the hat on his head.

"Now remember, Daddy, the idea is to catch five Ping-Pong balls in that bowl," Katie told him. "I wanted to use raw eggs like they do on the show, but Mommy wouldn't let me."

"Ping-Pong balls are fine," her dad assured her.

"You guys ready down there?" Becky called from her spot in the tree.

"Do you have your stopwatch on?" Katie asked Kevin.

He nodded.

"Okay!" Katie shouted up to Becky. "Start throwing them."

Becky started throwing the Ping-Pong balls down from the tree. Katie's dad ran around the playground, trying to catch them in the bowl on the top of his head.

"Time!" Kevin called out. "How many have you got in there, Mr. Carew?"

Katie's dad took the hat off of his head. "One," he said sadly. "On the show you have to catch five to stay in the game."

"Yeah, but on the show you'll have to catch real eggs," Katie reminded him. "They won't bounce out of the bowl the way Ping-Pong balls do."

"I guess," Mr. Carew said, brightening slightly.

"My turn!" Jeremy shouted. He walked over to a nearby picnic table and placed a plastic bowl on the table. There was green Jell-O in it.

"I put a jelly bean in the bowl," Jeremy told Katie's dad. "All you have to do is find the jelly bean. But you can't use your hands."

"And just to be sure you don't, we're going to tie your hands behind your back," Suzanne said. She took out a piece of pink ribbon and used it to tie up Mr. Carew's hands.

"Okay," Mr. Carew said. He started to stick his face into the bowl.

"No, see, that's where everybody goes wrong," Jeremy told him. "You don't shove your whole face in the bowl. That makes it hard to breathe. You should use your tongue and mouth to lick up the goo as fast as you can."

"That's a good tip," Katie said.

"Thanks," Jeremy answered. "I got the idea watching my cat, Lucky."

"I hope *I'm* lucky on Monday," Mr. Carew groaned before he started slurping up the Jell-O.

Chapter 15

Lub dub. Lub dub. Lub dub.

Katie's heart was pounding really hard as she sat in the television studio on Monday night.

Her mom squeezed her hand. "I'm so nervous," her mom said.

Her dad had worked really hard all weekend. He'd even moved a few feet on the roller skates. But if the stunt wheel landed on the unicycle, he was done for.

X X X

"Okay, Dave, are you ready?" Bob Ritchey asked Katie's dad once the show started.

"As ready as I'll ever be," Mr. Carew

answered. After all the exercise that he'd gotten, Mr. Carew had had two good nights of sleep.

Katie's dad spun the wheel. Around and around it went and came to a stop on the bowl of goo.

"He's good at this!" Katie whispered excitedly to her mother.

Bob Ritchey waved his hands and the curtain behind him opened. A table and chair appeared on the stage. Behind them was the Tick Tock Clock.

"That bowl on the table is filled with green goo," Bob Ritchey told Katie's dad. "Somewhere in the bottom of that bowl is a jelly bean. You have to find that jelly bean . . . with your tongue!"

Katie's dad looked out into the audience and winked at Katie. "No problem, Bob," Mr. Carew said happily. "I can do this one with my hands tied behind my back!"

And that's exactly what happened. Mr. Carew managed to find that jelly bean—with six seconds to spare.

"Mmm. A red one. My favorite," he mumbled, holding the jelly bean between his teeth and smiling for the camera.

"Yeah, Daddy!" Katie cheered excitedly as the rest of the audience applauded.

"Great job, Dave," Bob Ritchey congratulated him. "Now let's see how you do with the next questions."

Katie's dad stood up, wiped off his face,

and went back behind the wooden stand. He placed his hand on the buzzer and got ready to play.

"Bronco, whip, freeze, stoop, and maze are all types of what game?" Bob Ritchey asked.

Elaine reached for her buzzer. But Katie's dad was faster. He buzzed in first.

"Tag," he said.

"Right, Dave!" Bob Ritchey cheered. "You're off to a good start today. Let's try another one. Which can go longer without water—a camel or a rat?"

Katie's dad slammed down his buzzer once again. "A rat," he said confidently.

"Right again, Dave," Bob cheered. "Now, what state is known as the Land of Enchantment?"

This time Elaine hit her buzzer first. "New Mexico," she said.

"Right, Elaine." Bob Ritchey smiled into the camera. "Well, folks, it looks like we've got an exciting game going here," he told the audience.

Chapter 16

"I'm sorry your dad didn't win on *Tick, Tock, Clock* last night," Jeremy said as he walked to school with Katie the next morning. "That Elaine was really, really smart."

"Thanks to you, he found that jelly bean really fast and stayed in the game," Katie replied.

"Your dad sure answered a lot of questions after that," Jeremy added. "I thought he was going to win."

"Elaine only beat him by two points," Katie said proudly. "It was really close. And anyhow, he got a great prize for coming in second," Katie continued. "A huge TV."

"So he can watch *Tick, Tock, Clock*, right?" Jeremy asked.

"Every night," Katie assured him with a grin. "He got a new baseball hat, too. It says *Tick, Tock, Clock*. He hasn't taken it off since they gave it to him. I think he may have slept in it."

"So now he has a new favorite hat to replace the one Suzanne glued to the bowl," Jeremy remarked.

As she walked onto the playground, Katie noticed that things had changed at school, too. For once, everyone seemed to be getting along. No one was showing off or bragging about how many bracelets they had.

Katie was glad of that. Between *Tick, Tock, Clock* and all those rubber bracelets, she'd definitely had enough of bragging.

"I think it's going to be a good day," she told Jeremy happily.

Just then, Suzanne strolled onto the play-ground. "Hi, everybody," she said, waving her hand in the air.

Katie looked over. Suzanne was wearing a small metal ring on each of her thumbs.

"Wow, those are cool!" Miriam Chan said, complimenting Suzanne. "Where did you get them?"

"At Hot Stuff," Suzanne said. "They just got them in."

"I know," George said as he held up his hands. "I've got four of them."

"Well, I'm getting *more* after school," Suzanne told him.

"Then we'll see each other at the store," George replied. "Because *I'm* getting more rings, too."

Katie shook her head. "Oh, no," she groaned. "Here we go again."

Trivia

How would you do if you were a contestant on *Tick, Tock, Clock*? See how many of these crazy questions you can answer. Then try them on your friends!

1. Where is the Baseball Hall of Fame located?

2. True or false: Butterflies taste with their feet.

3. What singer is known as the King of Rock and Roll?

4. In what country was spaghetti invented?

5. Which country is shaped like a boot?

6. Name the colors in the rainbow.

7. Which country has the most cats?

8. What do you call a bee's nest?

9. Who carved Pinocchio?

10. Does it take more muscles to smile or frown?

Answers:

1. Cooperstown, New York
2. True. Butterflies' taste buds are on the bottoms of their feet.
3. Elvis Presley
4. China
5. Italy
6. Red, orange, yellow, green, blue, indigo, violet
7. The United States
8. A hive
9. Geppetto
10. Frown. You use forty-three muscles to frown but only seventeen to smile.